D1130652

Kali and
the Golden Mirror

By Eva-Lis Wuorio

KALI AND THE GOLDEN MIRROR

TAL AND THE MAGIC BARRUGET

THE LAND OF RIGHT UP AND DOWN

THE ISLAND OF FISH IN THE TREES

Kali and
the Golden Mirror

EVA-LIS WUORIO

illustrated by

EDWARD ARDIZZONE

The World Publishing Company

Cleveland and New York

Published by The World Publishing Company
2231 West 110th Street, Cleveland, Ohio 44102
Published simultaneously in Canada by
Nelson, Foster & Scott Ltd.
Library of Congress catalog card number: 67-13817
Text copyright © 1967 Eva-Lis Wuorio
Illustrations copyright © 1967 Edward Ardizzone

For my friend
KATIE HARRIS
with love

Chapter One

KALI came down the ancient hill with a tall woven basket on her shoulder. She skipped down the steep path on her bare feet. She didn't have to look down to avoid the rocks. She knew them all.

Below, the beach curved long and bright as far as the horizon. Nearly. There was just the thinnest line of deep blue beyond the far headland.

Closer, the sea came in to the bright sands, clear turquoise and pale blue. Further out, a wayward wind streaked the waves with purple and black. On the rocks by a small outer island, the spray broke into sparkling pearls. Kali smiled. She loved the sea.

The basket was heavy, but Kali was used to carrying it. She was thin and wiry and tanned by the sun. Her black short hair swung behind her ears and her long legs seemed longer because the faded blue smock was too short.

Usually Kali sang and whistled when she returned from

9

shopping in the high village. She was always happy to come back to the little white house in the dunes. There was such a warm welcome for her, and a mug of goat's-milk as well.

But today her bright brown eyes were serious. She didn't even hum. She was thinking hard.

It wasn't like thinking of the sea and how lovely it was. Nor like one's early morning thoughts of trying to figure out by the sound of the shutters what sort of day it was going to be. It wasn't a thought like, "I wonder if Uncle Kristo has had a good catch today," nor, "I wonder if Aunt Maria is going to make spicy rolls from the fig leaves I brought her."

Today her mind was churning with a problem. That was something new and much more difficult.

She had already figured out *what* she wanted to do. And *why* she wanted to do it.

Up until half an hour ago she just simply hadn't been able to think of *how* she was going to do it.

Now she saw a way. In a way, she saw it. But it still was all very difficult. Indeed it was.

Carefully she lowered the basket from her shoulder to her knee. Then she slid it to the ground. There was a handy boulder to sit on. She sat on it and picked a thorn out of her big toe.

She sat there quite a long time, a worried little dot in the immensity of brightness of a Greek morning.

"*Kali imara, mikro* Kali." It was a very kindly voice that surprised her out of her deep thought. "*Ti simvéni?* What is the matter, little Kali?"

A tall thin man slowly lowered himself down to the boulder beside the little girl. His hair was quite white, his face was brown and lined, and his dark eyes were friendly.

10

Kali jumped up and curtsied.

"*Kalimera,* Kyrios Virgilio," she smiled at him. *Kalimera* means good morning, and *Kyrios* means Mister. As they lived on the island of Skyros, which is in the northern Aegean Sea, they naturally spoke in Greek.

"Nothing is really the *matter,* dear Kyrios," she assured him. "It is just that I have a problem."

"Would it help to tell me about it?"

Kyrios Virgilio had retired as the schoolmaster on the island, but he still took great interest in the children and they loved him.

"As you perhaps know," Kali said seriously. "I am an orphan."

Kyrios Virgilio nodded his head gravely. He did know, but if Kali wanted to talk, he was ready to listen.

"My Thia Maria and my Thios Kristo have taken care of me since I was a baby," Kali continued.

"Indeed, your aunt and uncle have loved you well," the tall old man agreed.

"Now, it so happens," Kali said in her serious way, "that their tenth wedding anniversary will be soon. It will also be the anniversary of the day they took me as their very own Kali into their home."

The schoolmaster remembered. Ten years didn't seem as long a time to him as it did to Kali.

It had been a calm clear evening when the young fisherman Yanni and his wife had set out in their boat to lay their nets and lobster traps. They had perhaps sailed on in the moonlight, for a sudden storm, so usual in this sea, had caught them. They had not come back. Yanni's brother, Kristo, and his wife, Maria, had accepted the baby Kali into their care, on their own wedding day.

"Yes, little one," the schoolmaster said. "I remember."

"I love them well," Kali said.

"They too love you," the schoolmaster knew it was true.

"So," Kali said, "I have planned to give them a special gift on their anniversary. A splendid gift for them to see each morning as they awaken, to remind them of me."

"I see."

"Only, for a gift," Kali explained, "one needs money."

"True. True indeed," the schoolmaster agreed. He wondered how he could help.

"So I have decided to earn some," Kali said. "Only, it is a bit difficult, you see."

"Indeed it is," the schoolmaster knew that among the island

12

people there were very few *drachmas* (which is the Greek money) to spare for anything but necessities. It would be difficult to find work, because most of the people did their own chores. He said, "Would you like to come and tidy my books for me? And sweep and dust, perhaps?"

Kali's eyes sparkled. She laughed with joy. "Oh, you *are* kind, Kyrios," she said, "but I know as well as you that old Anna does all that for you. No, no, I must find my own way. Don't you see, that is part of the gift. For me to do it truly, myself."

The old schoolmaster was pleased. His face showed it.

"You are right, child," he said. "Of course you are right."

He got up and helped Kali lift the shopping basket onto her shoulder. They walked down the hill together until a path branched left. It led through the oleanders and into rush-grown valley of a little stream, where the schoolmaster had his house. Kali's way was down to the beach, to the little white house in the dunes.

"*Efharisto*, Kyrios," Kali said. "Thank you, Kyrios, it has been a great help to talk to you."

"*Parakaló, parakaló*," Kyrios Virgilio said. "Please, please, it is nothing. You will come and talk to me again, and tell me how you get on. And don't forget the little task I set you. What was it about?"

Kali knew he was testing her and said quickly, "I was to learn the legend of the hero Achilles, who was hidden in Skyros by his mother."

"Quite right, my child. Learn it, and when you know it, come and recite it to me. It is good to know the stories of one's own island."

13

As they parted Kali stared thoughtfully after the thin tall figure. Achilles! Why hadn't she thought of that before! Now she knew the way!

She skipped all the way home, singing.

Chapter Two

CARLOS

AUNT MARIA had hung a line of washing out in the bright sun. Against the white walls of the little house and the long white sand, the blue shirts of Uncle Kristo and the blue smocks of Kali and the striped aprons and skirts of Aunt Maria fluttered like butterflies.

She herself stood in the doorway and waved to Kali.

"*Kalóstone*," she called. She always called "Welcome!" to Kali when the little girl came home. "Did you get everything? Was there any news in the village? You were a long time gone!"

Kali hugged her. Her eyes sparkled. She was full of her new idea. Could she ever keep it a secret?

"I met Kyrios Virgilio on the way and we had a talk. And he wants me to do my task. And I did get everything, Aunt Maria. And do you know, the foreigners have come back. The foreigners who dig in the earth for old things."

"Have they! Oh, have they indeed. They will surely buy

15

And such a present would surely show Aunt Maria and Uncle Kristo how much she loved them. They always thought of her!

Why, only a year ago, Uncle Kristo had one day started to build something again. Kali had thought he was making a shed for his fishing gear, and the boat. But instead, it was a new room—as high as the rest of the little house, a narrow small room with a window looking back toward the valley of fig trees and the oleanders, and the cypress at the bottom of the conical hill of the village.

It would be for some special guest, Kali had thought. She had helped to whitewash it, and had watched Uncle Kristo build the low bed, carve the posts at the head of it, and build a neat shelf under the window. There was even a new blanket for the bed, a very gaily striped one, and curtains for the window.

It was the nicest little room Kali had ever seen. A guest would surely be pleased with it.

But on the morning of her name day Aunt Maria and Uncle Kristo had opened the door of the little room and shouted, "Many years, dear Kali! May you live many years!" This is what is said in Greece on your name day, which is the day of the saint for whom you are named.

"It is for me?" Kali hadn't been able to believe it.

"It is your room, child!"

So that was the room where Kali kept the few treasures she had, including the book that Kyrios Virgilio, the schoolmaster, had lent her.

She washed her hands first. Books were precious things, and she handled them carefully. Then she ran to her room.

18

It was a big old book, with yellowing pages, large print, and faded pictures. She knew the chapter she wanted.

Quickly she scanned the pages. She wanted to find one particular paragraph.

She remembered quite well reading that in the ancient times, beyond memory, Locomedes had been the King of the little island of Skyros. In those days the Greeks believed in mythical beings called Fates. The Fates were something like the people who write horoscopes today, purporting to know what is going to happen in the future. The ancient Greeks had believed very firmly in such predictions.

One of the many people who believed in what the Fates predicted was a Princess called Thetis. She had a son named Achilles, and the Fates had said that if he went to war against the city of Troy, he would be killed. If he stayed at home, however, he would live a long and dull life.

The Fates had also predicted that he would be famous throughout centuries if he did go to this war, but Thetis, being a mother, decided that she wanted for her son a long life instead of fame.

So she spoke to a friend of hers, the King of Skyros, and asked him whether Achilles could hide in his court.

Kali found the place in her book. It was the paragraph on just *how* Achilles had been hidden. She read it carefully again.

It was just as she had remembered. Achilles' mother had hidden him by dressing him up as a girl!

Kali read that part over again.

That was it. A disguise. Achilles, a boy of thousands of years ago, on this very island, had been disguised as a girl.

All right then, what would be wrong with her disguising herself as a boy?

Particularly when it was in such a good cause!

She put the book carefully back on the shelf.

Then she ran out.

"Aunt Maria," she called. "Will you please cut my hair short, the way you always do it for the summer?"

Chapter Three

THROUGHOUT the night the sea rushed up the beach. It made a symphony that sounded like "Whoomp-baaaaah-whooooooooooosh." A sort of sad blue sound.

The wind from Turkey blew the sand into whirls, and that made music too. It sounded like, "Sssssheeeeeesh-rrrrrrrat-tat-taaa-shoom."

Beyond, in the valley of the little river, the olive trees and the fig trees, the oleanders and the cane, sang their own song. A green whispering song, as opposed to the song of the Turkish wind, which was gold and rust.

When one lives in a very small house in the dunes, as Kali did, all these sounds become familiar. Even on the night of the strongest, loudest wind, they are not frightening. Kali listened to them, comfortably snug in her bed, and tried to plan ahead.

She would need some boys' clothes. That was a problem, all right.

Well. She'd not worry. Aunt Maria always said, "Every morning is a new beginning." She'd wait for the morning.

And the morning came bright and high blue. While Kali was still sweeping the kitchen there was a cheerful shout outside.

"Hérete! Kaliméra!"

It was the kind voice of the doctor's wife calling, "Hello, here I am! Good morning!"

Kali threw down the broom and ran out.

"Yásas!" she cried, which means, "Health to you!" and is a correct greeting. But then she remembered, and curtsied and said, *"Kalós orísate,"* because that was more polite, although it meant just the same thing.

"There you are, little Kali. The doctor's wife had a happy smile. "Come and help me. Is your Aunt Maria about?"

Kali rushed up with a low wooden stool, and the doctor's wife skipped lightly onto it, and off the donkey. She was small herself, so she liked to have a stool to get down from the little animal. There were woven baskets and bags tied about the donkey's neck and rump.

Aunt Maria ran out, wiping her hands on her apron.

They all said good-morning, and health to you, and live long, in the polite way the Greek people have, and then they admired the brilliant morning. Every day, almost, in Greece, the light is like sparkling spring water, and the sun is newly washed, the sky bright shining blue. All the same, every day people stop to admire the beautiful day.

When all that was done, the doctor's wife said, "As you know, Maria, I have sisters and cousins in America. They kindly send me parcels of American things now and then.

22

This time I have something that you might not like Kali to wear. All the same, I do assure you, all the little girls in America do wear these things."

She began to unpack one of her baskets.

"Here is a dress for you, Maria. Here are some shirts for Kristo."

Then she pulled out brown shorts and blue jeans, and sweaters and shirts. "Look," she said, "these do look like boys' clothes, but really all the little girls in America wear them. I thought they might do for Kali, for the summer. She *is* growing out of her smocks, isn't she?"

"You are sure, Kyria," Aunt Maria asked, "that these really are clothes for little *girls?*"

"Oh, yes. I can show you pictures in the magazines they also send me. These are summer clothes for playing, and working, and for the beach."

"Well, a lot of beach we certainly have, and work as well," said Aunt Maria, "so thank you with my heart. Kali shall wear them."

"Thank you!" Kali skipped about. Her face was radiant. Her problem was solved. Perhaps the Fates were at work! Even though she wasn't an ancient Greek.

"You can put them on now if you wish, child," the doctor's wife laughed. It was just the right kind of morning to see a happy child.

Kali could hear them talking while she was in her little room changing into the clothes she had so wished for. It really was the best of luck. Luck, or Fates, or dear God who had heard her wish.

The doctor's wife was saying, "Maria, there is also a favor

23

I wish to ask you. At long last my husband has time to take a holiday. Apollo, this old donkey of ours, does not like many people, but he is familiar with you and Kristo and Kali. Would you do me the kindness to look after him while we are away?"

"Of course, Kyria," Aunt Maria cried. "We will be glad to have him with us. Kali will tether him in the shadow of the fig tree and if there is rain or storm he can sleep in the kitchen."

"Please, also, let him do some work. He can take Kali up to the village when she goes shopping. He likes to go to the village. Only, he is old, so ask her not to make him go too fast."

"I'll never do that." Kali came running out. "I'll walk beside him and help him." She put her arms around old Apollo's neck.

24

Aunt Maria clapped her hands. "My goodness! You look just like a little boy!"

Kali laughed and agreed.

That was what she had hoped she would look like.

Surely now she could get a job with the foreigners digging in the earth for old things. Surely now she could earn enough to buy the Golden Mirror.

The doctor's wife was saying to Aunt Maria, "Why don't you sell Kristo's lobster and fish, and the vegetables from your patch in the valley, to the foreigners up at the excavations? They are there again digging for ancient relics."

"What is the good of all that?" Aunt Maria asked curiously.

"It is to help re-create the past. Sometimes it proves our old legends are true, in a sense. But mainly, these old finds teach us how people lived long ago, what sort of people they were, what kind of things they did, what they had in their houses. The past is part of our present, you see."

"And what is the use of *that*, my lady?" Aunt Maria asked. "We have the problem of trying to make our living today."

"The things in the past make a sort of song, my aunt," Kali said. It was not polite to interrupt the conversation of your elders, but she had become very much interested. "It is a song of all the things that have always been. I am sure even Achilles sometimes comes back to Skyros."

"Achilles, the hero from the long past!" Aunt Maria clapped her hands. "That child! She says the most extraordinary things at times!"

"It is a fine thing to have imagination," the doctor's wife said. "Kali is right. Our past is a brave song. Greece must remain proud of the greatness that once was ours. If we remember it we'll once again be great."

She leaned against the pillar of the little patio and talked as though to herself. "We never conquered anything except the hearts and minds of mankind. We still have the ability to do the same thing, as long as we have children like Kali, growing up here, on the sand dunes by a fisherman's beach, on the island of Skyros."

She smiled at Aunt Maria. "Let Kali and Apollo deliver the fish to the camp of the foreigners. There is much she can learn up there about our own history. It is a useful way to spend a summer."

Chapter Four

EARLY in the morning Kali was up. This was the day she would start her "labors." (In ancient Greek legends the great heroes always called their adventurous tasks "labors.")

It had been a rainy night, so Apollo, the donkey, had slept in the big old kitchen. Kali led him out into the morning brightness. She had found an old brush, and Aunt Maria had said she could also use a broken comb that was going to be thrown away anyway.

The shaggy old donkey stood patiently while Kali combed and brushed him. He really was an extremely ragged-looking old creature. His ears flopped and his upper lip curled in a fierce way. Only people who loved him would recognize this expression as a smile. To most others it looked like a snarl. He had been called Apollo, not as a joke, but to make him feel better about not being very beautiful. Donkeys are wise. Probably the kind thought about his name had made him such an amiable beast.

27

Uncle Kristo had put his choicest lobsters into a basket. Aunt Maria had selected her best tomatoes and fresh sweet peppers. Kali had collected the new-laid eggs and these were carefully put into a wicker hamper.

"I am not sure at all about these clothes, little Kali," Aunt Maria said. "I don't like to have a little girl go about in trousers." She helped Kali to hang the baskets on Apollo so that they wouldn't bother him.

"They are very comfortable," Kali assured her. "And very warm."

That did the trick. There was a brisk wind blowing, and Aunt Maria had her shawl about her head, one end of it in her mouth to keep it firm. She always worried about the wind because Kali wouldn't wear shawls. (Except in the winter.)

So Kali and Apollo set off into the golden day. In the val-

28

ley beyond the dunes the little river lirrupped, the rushes rustled, and birds sang in the oleanders. The path climbed up to where the hill became barren and brown. Kali skirted the village and led the donkey upwards. There was not much to mark the way, for rain had washed away the loose earth, sun had bleached the stones, and winds had swept for centuries. But Kali knew which way to go.

Finally they came to a high headland. The sun was high in the sky and the air sparkled. The tents of the foreigners looked small in the vastness of it all.

Apollo slowed down. Kali was sure he knew how shy she felt. It would be difficult to speak to the strangers. She'd met only a few in her life.

Right then a tall man crawled out of the closest tent. He wore a white shirt, faded trousers, and sandals, and his face was burned red by the sun. His hair was fair and his eyes were blue and friendly.

"Good morning," he said cheerily, in Greek. "And what have we here? Our first guest, and welcome to you!"

He knew the right greeting.

"Kalós sás vríkame," Kali said politely.

Apollo trotted over. There was a prickly bush near the tent. He rather fancied the taste of it.

Kali fell off his back. She wasn't yet used to his sudden decisions. The tall man hauled her up in a friendly way.

"You have brought us something in your baskets?" he asked.

"Lobsters," Kali said, "my Uncle Kristo brought them in from the bay this morning. Eggs—they are fresh too. And some tomatoes, please."

"Well, let me see," said the tall man. "We'll be glad to have them, I'm sure. Bunty!" he called. "Come and see!"

A very slim woman came out of the biggest of the tents. She looked like a boy herself, Kali thought, in her jeans and her shirt, except for the fact that she had long coppery hair tied with a ribbon at the nape of her neck. Her eyes were green and she had freckles.

"How nice," she said. "Food."

She gave her hand to Kali. Her Greek was a little odd, her words were not in quite the right order, nor did she say them with the right sort of accent, but her smile was so friendly Kali understood her.

"How are you?" She really seemed to mean it. "What is your name, little boy?"

"I am well, and I wish you health," Kali said. "I am Kali."

Her hands flew to her mouth. She'd said *Kali!* A girl's name. And all her plans depended on the foreigners' thinking she was a boy!

"Those are lovely lobsters." The slim woman was digging into Kali's baskets. "And excellent eggs."

She hadn't seemed to notice Kali's slip of the tongue at all. Perhaps she didn't know that Kali stood for Calliope, which in Greek means a beautiful voice. Kali's mother had been so enchanted to hear her baby's first cry, Aunt Maria had often told Kali, that she'd decided right away to call her Calliope. Kali loved to hear that story.

"There is another thing," Kali said.

"Yes?" Both the foreigners stopped looking into the baskets and turned to listen to her. They seemed to be very nice people.

"There was a notice in the *kafenion* window. Yesterday morning I saw it," Kali explained. "I read it myself, although

30

slowly, for the printing was strange; it said that you had need for a boy to help with the work. I am that boy, please."

The two foreigners looked at one another.

Then the man said, "You are very little, you know. We need a boy to clean up, and carry earth, and sort the earth carefully, and take messages."

"I am very strong," Kali said. Her voice shook. "I am very strong," she said again, hanging her head.

The slim woman was staring at her, hard. But her eyes were soft.

Kali decided to have another try. "And I am very careful," she said firmly. "Did I break a single one of those eggs on the way here? And the path is rough."

"And you very much want to work with us? Why?"

They looked so kind, both of them. Kali knew that if she

"And you really boiled the lobsters for them, child? You remembered everything?"

"Yes, I did, Aunt Maria," Kali said. "Apollo and I went up to the little spring you showed me, and there we got the herbs, as you taught me. Apollo ate well, too, of the grass and thistles. And I used spring water, and sea salt from the rocks."

"But what interests *me*," said Uncle Kristo, "is what they are *doing*. Digging trenches into the hillside like that. I just don't understand it at all. I know they have permission, and I know the big officials seem to approve of them, but what do they do it for? What are they looking for?"

"Perhaps for a treasure," Aunt Maria said. "For gold and diamonds and things like that."

"No," Kali said, staring into the fire. "I don't think it's

like that at all." She tried to explain, "Gently, carefully, they sift the earth, and when there is even a smallest crumb, like a broken piece of an old jug, they are happy. They shout to one another and say, 'Look what I've found! This must be the right site!' And I must put the earth into plastic bags, and mark the place it came from, and they put out strings, and pegs, and keep measuring all the time, and drawing maps. And I must be very careful of every *handful* of earth I touch."

"Why, Kali, were you working with them?"

"Well, as a matter of fact," Kali grinned, "I was. It was very interesting, and you did say I did not have to hurry home."

"It is a kindness to help the foreigners," said Uncle Kristo.

Kali blushed. Her bread stuck in her throat. She said, "They will pay me for my work, Uncle Kristo."

"Good angels in the high sky!" Aunt Maria cried. "That is not possible. Whatever a little girl like you can do to help, it is only right for you to do. They are, after all, visitors to our island, and we must try to make them welcome. And besides, they buy the fish Kristo brings from the sea, the fruits from my little plot, which is a blessing."

"Your aunt is right," Uncle Kristo said.

"But," Kali said. And couldn't go on. How was she going to explain that she was working to get them an anniversary present? After all, it had to be a surprise. And she couldn't explain either that the foreigners had put up a notice to say they needed a boy to work for them, whom they were willing to pay. She couldn't say she had lied—well, she hadn't exactly *said* she was a boy, but she had not said she wasn't, when they supposed she was. Aunt Maria would call that prevarication, and be both sad and angry.

35

Now she would have to prevaricate at home too.

Kali wished she had someone to talk to about it all. But would any grown-up understand her problem? She would have to think about it.

Uncle Kristo, luckily, did not notice Kali's preoccupation. He was still thinking of the curious digging the foreigners were doing. He mopped up the rest of his stew with a piece of bread and poured himself some *retzina,* in a small blue enamel mug. It was good for the stomach.

"Tell me again, then, of these people, little Kali," he asked, feeling warm and full and content. He was a wiry, dark man who looked as though he never ate much. But he had a very good appetite.

"It is like this," Kali said, "There is Kyrios Malcolm. The sun has burned his face, and the blue sky has made his eyes the same color as itself. He is very tall, but not as broad as you, Uncle Kristo. His hair is yellow. He folds himself up into three when he kneels in the trenches to dig, and when he measures out the string for new work. He has many books and strange instruments in his tent. He also photographs everything, the old works from last year, the new strings, the tiny pieces of broken pottery in the earth. Just as though it were a wedding."

In all her life Kali had seen photographers only at weddings.

"Then," she continued, "there is Kyria Bunty. She is very thin but she looks healthy. She has hair the color of fire, in the sun. She wears clothes just like mine."

"You don't mean to tell me!" Aunt Maria cried. "A lady wearing clothes like yours!"

"Yes, like these that the doctor's wife gave me. Just this

36

same sort of pants, only bigger, naturally, for her. And she has many curious things in her cook-tent, and many books also. She is the wife of Kyrios Malcolm."

"Just the two of them?" Aunt Maria asked. "And all that hillside to dig up?"

"Some others are coming. Last night they were going to the harbor to meet the boat from Kymi. That is why they were so glad to have the lobsters. That is why they will need more things every day."

"Oh? But you should have stayed to keep the lobsters warm for them!"

"They said they would eat them cold."

"I will go myself to see these strangers," Uncle Kristo said. "Then we will know if it is all right for Kali to stay late some night to keep the lobsters warm for them."

Uncle Kristo loved Kali.

"And truly it is not for a treasure they dig?" Aunt Maria persisted.

"No," Kali said again. "Once upon a time, it seems, there was a great town with a mighty palace on that bare hill of ours. They want to dig down to find out what it may have looked like. Kyria Bunty told me that from the little broken things found in the earth one could figure out what the people in ancient times did, what they wore, how they cooked, everything like that. So that is why they dig."

"I see," Aunt Maria said, "they try to see the past. Only it seems to me it would be much simpler just to listen to the sea, just to look at each morning dawning. These are the same as they were long ago. Everything has always been the same, here in Greece."

"Perhaps," Uncle Kristo said, "and perhaps not."

Kali fed a carrot to Apollo and went to bed. She was tired but she was happy. Despite the worrying prevarications she had, after all, started on her "labor." Just like the heroes of the ancient legends.

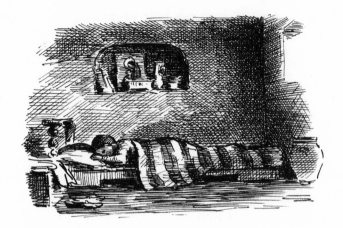

Chapter Six

THE DAYS flew by. And the weeks flew by. The clear translucent Greek spring blinded the eyes with beauty. Kali and Apollo went up the hill each early morning with fresh vegetables, eggs, and milk. Uncle Kristo caught fabulous fish. The little trenches began to show a pattern of a small ancient town, with places for streets and colonnades, market places and temples.

If you didn't know what it was all about, it seemed only a haphazard puzzle in the dry brown earth. But when you understood it to be the plan of an old city, slowly being rediscovered, it was fascinating.

Sometimes, too, the diggers would find little bronze statues of men, and birds, and mythical creatures. Or there would be terra-cotta figurines or a fragment of pottery painted with care and artistry hundreds and hundreds of years ago.

On days of these happy discoveries Uncle Kristo would come up with his best lobster, or a big *synagrida*, which is

39

a sea bass, or a *barbounia,* or even with octopus and squid, shrimps and prawns. And Aunt Maria too would come up to cook *garides pilaffi,* or *kalamaráki,* and always *dolmas,* which is a dish of vine leaves stuffed with ground meat and rice, and which was the favorite of Kyrios Malcolm.

Kali had almost forgotten her problems and worries. When Uncle Kristo first came up to see what the foreigners were like, she was afraid that her secret would be discovered.

However, everyone called her Kali. No one had thought to ask whether she was a girl or a boy. And Uncle Kristo had liked Kyrios Malcolm and Kyria Bunty, so all was well.

It was the same when Kyrios Virgilio, the kindly schoolmaster, climbed up to the digs. He was so interested in everything, and so pleased that Kali should learn about the history of her own island first hand, that he didn't notice anything strange either.

Many people from the village came too, for they were curious about the goings on. After all, it was their own ancient history the foreigners were kindly digging up. And all the little treasures would go to their own National Museums, if not in Skyros, at least in the great white capital of Athens.

Kali had had the problem about her wages too.

After the first week Kyrias Bunty had said to her, "You may *look* little, small Kali, but you work at least double your size. Here is your pay, and you are well worth it."

Kali didn't know what to do. It was the first money she had ever earned. It seemed like a great deal. But it wasn't for her, it was for the Anniversary Present. She couldn't put out her hand to touch it.

Finally she said, "Please, Kyria. Will you keep it for me? We could put it into a bowl in the cook tent."

40

(Aunt Maria always kept her egg money, or whatever she earned from helping people, or from selling the vegetables from her garden, in an earthen bowl on a shelf in the kitchen.)

"Are you sure you don't want it now? To take home, to show to your family?"

"I am quite sure," Kali said. "Thank you, Kyria. Please to keep it for me until I have enough."

The slim woman with the copper hair was quite Greek in her politeness. She didn't ask, "To keep until you have enough for what?" No, not at all. She simply went into the cook tent and she found a brown earthenware bowl, and she put Kali's wages into that. Then she put it back on the shelf next to the coffee and tea tins. She said, "That's yours. To take any time you wish."

And the days flew by, shining bright and brilliant blue.

Everyone was happy working. After all, the foreigners were there because they wanted to do what they were doing. Uncle Kristo liked to fish, even if it was dangerous sometimes with the winds and the sudden storms. Aunt Maria liked to keep her house tidy and Uncle Kristo and Kali happy. Kyrios Virgilio loved his books and the ancient island. And Kali and Apollo simply loved each shining day. What a spring it was!

But there *was* one shadow: this business of not having told all the truth, neither to the kind foreigners, nor to her aunt and uncle.

During the happy days she would forget about it. But at night when she awakened with the moon making paths across her little room, it did worry her.

Then there came the evening when Uncle Kristo had brought fresh fish to the camp, and was waiting to walk home with Kali. (Apollo never walked any faster, if he didn't want to and mostly he didn't, than the slowest human being.)

While everyone was still admiring the new finds of the day—just some pieces of pottery and the rusted handle of a sword—the man from the post office in the village below pushed his bicycle up the cliff. You couldn't ride a bicycle on that rough path, but it made him feel more business-like to arrive with a bicycle.

"A telegram," he said. "I hope with all my heart it is not bad news. I thought to leave it until tomorrow if it was bad, but then again, I thought it could be good, so I hurried. With my bicycle."

"Thank you, *efharisto*, thank you," Kyrios Malcolm said, and tore open the envelope. "Why," he cried, "how splendid! Some of our friends are arriving on their boat tonight. Oh Kristo, could we have more lobsters, do you think?"

42

"I came here first," Uncle Kristo said, "so you could have the first choice. Here is a sackful. I was going to leave the rest in the village, but perhaps you will take me down to Linaria with you and I'll sell them there."

"I'll stay here to cook them, and get everything ready," Kyria Bunty said to her husband. "You go to meet the boat."

"Oh, no, you must come too," Kyrios Malcolm cried. "They'd expect to see you at the port."

"I'd like to come," Kyria Bunty smiled regretfully, "but there is so much to do here."

Uncle Kristo stepped forward. He said, "Kyrios Malcolm, Kyria Bunty, please to permit my small Kali to do this service for you. If there is anything else you need for the feast of your friends I will bring it up myself."

"I've got everything here, Uncle Kristo," Kali said. "Lemon and oil for the sauce, and the peppers and tomatoes and rice, and I will make *taramasalata* to begin with. Aunt Maria also sent up fresh bread this morning. I will be glad to do it."

"But you will be here alone in the camp, and we shall not be back until long after dark." Kyria Bunty looked worried. The helpers lived down in the village and they had already left.

"That is all right," Kali said. "I love this place."

"It is all right," Uncle Kristo said. He had made sure about the foreigners before he let Kali work for them. He also was sure that on this small island of good people, nothing strange could happen.

Chapter Seven

KALI lit a fire under the outside grill. If she made it small to begin with it would burn long and get very hot. She put the large iron kettle on top of the grill and filled it with spring water.

In the cook tent she got out all the herbs, vegetables, oil, vinegar, lemons, and spices she would need. It was easy to cook when you knew what things you were going to use. Aunt Maria always said, "Get everything out before you start, then you don't have to go searching for the salt when the pot's already boiling."

While there was still the light of the evening glow she made a camp bed for herself in the cook tent. Kyria Bunty had left her fragrant sheets and blankets. The foreigners had taken to the Greek way of airing things on pine trees and on the small bushes of thyme and rosemary.

When she had everything ready, everything she could possibly think of, she pulled a little stool close to the fire and sat

44

down. She would add wood to it slowly, until it was time to start cooking.

The sky was purple-blue and seemed closer than during the day. The stars leaned down. This was the time to speak to them. When the moon came up, the stars would go further away.

Kali thought to herself, her chin in her hands, her elbows on her knees, what a splendid spring it had been.

Apollo was such a loving donkey. Kali and he had a wonderful time together, jogging through the valley and up the hill each early shining morning. The money the foreigners paid for the fish and the eggs and the vegetables had in turn paid for the new nets Uncle Kristo had had to get to replace the ones he had lost in the winter storms. The foreigners had taught her words of English, and they had allowed her to

45

letter the little bags for the fragments of pottery, lost so long in the ancient sands. Perhaps now the people of the past somehow knew that they were no longer forgotten.

It had grown quite dark.

Kali got up to feed the fire. Soon the coals would be just right for the slow cooking of the casserole of vegetables. It must be past midnight, Kali judged from the height of the moon. She must have been half asleep for the time to have gone so fast.

Moonlight was strange.

It seemed to make arches and pillars on the headland. The shadows had grown solid, like buildings. Temples and palaces. And there was light, as from a huge open doorway.

The moon magic, of course, Kali thought. But it was strange, all the same. You could imagine you saw a street of houses. And even that you heard the sound of zithers.

"I must put the lobster pot on now," Kali said aloud to herself.

"Let me help you," a voice said. "I know a good way of cooking them."

Kali turned.

Behind her, smiling, his blond hair swinging over his forehead and nearly down to his shoulders, was a tall slender boy in a tunic.

Kali knew about tunics. Boys often wore them at the Games, when they were putting on a show about ancient times.

"I am Achilles," the tall boy said. "I came because you called me."

"I—I don't *think* I called you," Kali said. "Surely you are not the Achilles from the book?"

46

"I don't know what you mean by that." Now that Kali looked at him more carefully, he seemed taller and more serious. "I am Achilles, son of Peleus, King of the Myrmidons, and of the sea-goddess, Thetis."

Kali stared at him. "I've read about you," Kali said, "if you really are Achilles the hero who hid here in Skyros, and then went on to fight and win the battle of Troy."

The boy laughed. "That's a very funny way to put it. And what do you know about Troy? I'm only now making ready to leave for that war."

"But you have been hiding here, haven't you?" Kali insisted.

"And how did you know about that? It is supposed to be a secret." The tall boy wore a gold band on his head and his sandals were gold too. He was frowning.

"I told you," Kali said, "I read it in a book. Perhaps in a way I did call you, because there is something very important I want to ask you about."

"Yes?" the tall boy seemed puzzled.

"How did you feel about the lie? The lie that you were a girl, instead of a boy?" Kali asked. "My Aunt Maria and my Uncle Kristo have told me and told me that to lie is an evil thing. A sin, in fact."

"It wasn't my idea. It was my mother's," the boy snapped. Then he laughed. "It was all rather funny, really. And, you know, she did it because she thought she was saving me from some danger or other. But it never works."

"What do you mean?" Kali asked. "It never works?"

"A lie. You cannot carry a lie through life. The truth will always come out. That's what I mean," the boy said.

47

"I wonder what's going to happen to me then," Kali said. "I've got this job by pretending I was a boy, because I wanted to earn money to buy an anniversary present for my Aunt Maria and my Uncle Kristo who have always been good to me."

The fire grew stronger and blew light and shadow into the night around them. The sea below sounded like the church organ, boom, boom, in the dark keys.

"That was not really a lie," said the golden-haired boy. "You were trying to do a good deed, so that must be taken into account."

The fire flamed higher. Kali decided to move the big iron pot onto the bigger grill. Achilles helped her to lift it. Then both of them dropped the lobsters into it, and thyme, and sea salt, and a few peppery small pimientos. Soon it would

48

Chapter Eight

KALI rubbed her eyes again.

The dawn was flowing green and bright over the far edge of the sea. Only seconds before, it seemed to her, there had been moonlight, and the shadows of the colonnades, the dark mass of arches and towers, and Achilles.

She felt sure she hadn't slept. Why, the coals glowed in the ashes and the huge iron pot was bubbling. No, she couldn't have slept.

Yet, here it was dawn already. Up the hill climbed Kyrios Malcolm, Kyria Bunty, and a group of strangers. And a surprise, for Aunt Maria was with them too.

Kali jumped up. Her legs felt full of pins and needles.

"I'm well," she ran to meet them. "I am awake. The fire is hot. The water is boiling."

They came up the hill gaily, laughing, singing, and carrying the luggage, bags and bags of it. Aunt Maria began to

50

bustle about the cooking pots. The morning brightened. Kali curled up and went to sleep.

No one awakened her, because they thought she had done so bravely to watch at the site, and feed the fire, and wait for them all through the hours of the night. The boat had been very late because the sea had been rough, as it often is between the mainland and Skyros.

Everyone ate well, and they were all happy to be where they were, on the seaborne cliff in the bright Greek morning.

When Kali awoke, the visitors were opening their cases and bags. They had all sorts of strange and wonderful things. They also had presents, for Kyria Bunty had written to them about her Greek friends.

"Now here," said the lady visitor to Aunt Maria, "is a piece of material perhaps you will be good enough to accept." She knew that that was the way one said it, when giving gifts in Greece. "I come from Manchester, and we think there that we make the best dress material in the world."

"This is a knife from Finland, where I come from" said another visitor, "and a flashlight. Kali can choose."

"Look at this, Bunty," said the lady visitor. She held up a scarf that was the colours of the sea and sky, blue and green and turquoise. Kali couldn't take her eyes off it.

She reached out and touched it with her finger tips. It was soft. The colours sang.

Kyria Bunty laughed. Her laughter had a silvery sound.

"Oh, Kali, Kali," she said. "I don't think you could have fooled us very much longer. You are so gentle. You cook so well. Really, you aren't a little *boy* at all, are you?"

51

"What's this! What's this?" Aunt Maria was shocked. "*Of course* she isn't a boy. She is our Kali. She is the daughter of my husband's brother, who died too soon, too young. She is our own little girl."

"*That's* what Achilles meant," Kali thought aloud. "Why, that is just what happened to Achilles."

"What is it, child?" Aunt Maria cried. "Are you not well?"

"I know what she means," Kyria Bunty said. "She means that long ago, when Achilles was disguised as a girl and hiding in the palace that used to be on this cliff, he betrayed himself by taking up a sword rather than jewelry."

Everybody began to babble at once. As only Kali and Kyria Bunty knew what they were talking about, they had to explain.

"Just now, history repeated itself," Kyria Bunty said. "Kali wanted the scarf rather than the Finnish knife and so we discovered she was a girl, not a boy."

"Oh, *why* did you say you were a boy, child?" Aunt Maria burst into tears.

"They *wanted* a boy, don't you see," Kali tried to explain. "The notice in the coffee shop window said they wanted a *boy*. To work for them. That's why, my own Aunt Maria."

Aunt Maria dried her tears. She looked angry. "I am going to make the coffee now," she said. "You will explain to me later."

She swept off, her face stern.

There was a silence.

Finally, Kyria Bunty said, "Would you explain, little Kali, what it is you have been trying to do?"

"I set myself a task, do you see," Kali said. "Like the ancient heroes. They always did a 'labor.' They had to kill a monster or do something else that seemed impossible. Well, the first part of my labor was to earn some money. The only way I could do it was to pretend I was a boy so you would give me a job."

"Do you want the money now?" Kyria Bunty asked. "You know where it is. In the brown pot on the shelf."

"No, no!" Kali cried. "And please don't tell Aunt Maria about it."

Aunt Maria was coming from the cook tent with the coffee pot and cups on a tray. Kali rushed to set the folding table.

Kyria Bunty looked at her husband. She lifted her eyebrow.

Kyrios Malcolm said, "Don't fuss. Don't say anything. Our little Kali is not a selfish child. If she does not want her aunt

53

to know about the money she has earned, that's her business. Let it be."

"All the same, Malcolm," said Kyria Bunty, "I don't think it's good to let children prevaricate about things. Shouldn't we make Kali tell us, with her Aunt Maria here, what it's all about?"

"No," said her husband, smiling gently. "I've suspected she was a little girl ever since the first day she came. But she's worked well. It's her problem, whatever it is, and we will help her. But not until she asks us."

Kali said, "May I go now? Apollo would like to drink in the river. And there are fresh greens for him there by the water. Please?"

"I'll speak to you when I come home," Aunt Maria said, busily seeing that everyone had a mug of hot coffee.

Chapter Nine

KALI cried all the way home.

Aunt Maria had never before been angry with her in all her life.

It was a good thing the path from the archaeological site on the top of the Mount skirted the village. She didn't have to see anyone except the goatman with his herd of goats and his tall staff and his water-pipe whistle. The goatman simply nodded to her. He was always thinking of other things. Such as where in the arid hills he could find greens to feed his goats.

By the time Apollo and Kali got down to the valley, Kali was really miserable. She untethered Apollo and let him walk by himself. There were only empty baskets for her to carry anyhow.

"I'm going home," Kali said to Apollo. "You come when you've had enough to eat."

Uncle Kristo was sitting cross-legged outside the kitchen

door when she got home, mending his torn nets. He looked up and saw Kali's tear-stained face.

He was a kind man. He loved his little niece. So, first of all, he just said, "I feel a little hungry because I've been out at my nets since dawn. I'd like a mug of warm goat's-milk, Kali. You could use one too, after the walk down from the cliff."

Kali nodded. Words stuck in her throat.

When she brought out their mugs the morning was already brilliant clear blue. The sea piled against the clean white sands. Uncle Kristo put down his long needle threaded with thick rusty cord, and the net.

"Tell me what is the matter, little Kali." He always said things abruptly, but his voice was kind. "I don't like to see you unhappy."

"O!" Kali began to cry again. "It was supposed to be a surprise."

56

"Tell me, then?"

"But it was going to be a surprise for you too, Uncle Kristo," Kali said. "Now everything is spoiled."

Uncle Kristo leaned across and gave Kali a quick hug. "Tell me why."

"Because my own Aunt Maria is angry with me. And how can I explain! It won't be a surprise if I have to explain!"

"You can tell me, child," Uncle Kristo said. He got up and brought a fresh egg from the kitchen. He stirred it into Kali's milk. "You have been up all night, that's what's the matter with you. Just have a little breakfast and you'll be feeling better. All of us old fishermen know that one has to have a little something in the stomach to be able to face the day."

"Well, it's like this," Kali said. "Pretty soon it will be your tenth wedding anniversary."

"True enough," said Uncle Kristo. "I didn't think you'd remember. In fact, it is tomorrow."

"So I was going to get you a surprise. A present. A golden mirror like the one the traveling man showed us. Because I've loved you all these many, many years."

"I see," Uncle Kristo said. "I see it now."

"Yes. But of course I needed money for the present."

"Of course," Uncle Kristo said. "Anyone would."

"Which is the reason I did not tell the foreigners I was not a boy, do you see?"

"Not quite," Uncle Kristo said. "But never mind. Don't cry."

Kali's words came in a rush. She told him the whole tale, right from the beginning.

"And now it's all ruined," she cried. "Because it isn't a surprise."

57

"No. It isn't ruined," said Uncle Kristo. "I'll tell you what we'll do."

They had just finished making their plans when Aunt Maria came home.

She was very seldom angry. She was a very kind person. But this morning her mouth was in a tight line, and her eyes were troubled.

"We have breakfast ready for you, Aunt Maria," Kali said.

"A fresh piece of fish," Uncle Kristo said. "Taste it. I caught it specially for you."

Aunt Maria looked at them.

"You two have been up to something," she said. "But that doesn't excuse a little girl's lying about being a boy."

"I didn't *lie*," Kali said. "I just didn't say I wasn't."

"Same thing," Aunt Maria said.

"We'll leave all that for now." When Uncle Kristo spoke in his head-of-the-family voice, everyone listened. "Kali and I have a few things to do in the village."

He gave a hug to his wife, "It's our anniversary tomorrow," he whispered.

Apollo was meandering home as Kali and Uncle Kristo started up the hill to the village. He had been having a good time in the valley of the little river, and he was burping as he ambled.

"First things first," Uncle Kristo said to Kali.

"If you say that's the right thing to do," Kali said, "I'll do it."

So first of all they climbed up to the archaeological digs. Kali went right up to Kyria Bunty and Kyrios Malcolm and said, "I have come to tell you the truth."

58

They stopped working immediately. They put out folding chairs next to the cook tent. The sky was immeasurably high and very blue. The ancient mountain breathed its secrets.

Kali explained: all about her being an orphan, and the anniversary present, and why she had not said she wasn't a boy, and why now, at last, she would like her wages.

"You know where they are, Kali," Kyria Bunty said.

Kali fetched the brown earthenware jug from the shelf. She poured out the money that was in it. They counted it.

Uncle Kristo stood up. "It is entirely too much," he said. "Kali could not possibly have earned all this."

"Is it enough for my present?" Kali said.

"But where can we get it now, anyhow, dear Kali?" Uncle Kristo dropped back into his chair. "A mirror like that cannot be bought in our village."

"Tell me about it," said Kyria Bunty.

So Kali explained about the traveling man who had showed

59

them the mirror with the golden frame. And she talked about the room Uncle Kristo had made, and of her own room which was one of the many kind things she had been given.

(And somehow, as she talked, she seemed to remember that Achilles had showed her the palace beyond the colonnades, and a large high hall, with a golden mirror just like the one she wanted, on the wall. Could it have been true, what had happened in the night? Or had she only dreamed it?)

"Why, I know," Kyria Bunty said. "I've seen a mirror like that in a shop at Kymi. It's a copy of the old, old mirrors, found in excavations or in the sea, perhaps. They have used the ancient design."

"In that case there is no problem," said Kyrios Malcolm. "Our friends came in their own big boat. They will let us use it. The sea is calm today, so if we leave right away, we can do all the anniversary shopping over on the mainland."

The Anniversary

THERE is a high bare rock of an island, half an hour's sail away from the long silver shore where Kali lives with her Uncle Kristo and Aunt Maria.

On the rock is a tiny white chapel, with no windows because the sea would break them, and only one small door, firmly fastened. It is dedicated to the saint who looks after fishermen. It is the little chapel where Maria and Kristo had been married. For that reason the kindly old priest had promised to go there with them again, on their tenth anniversary.

They went in several boats, the blue sails billowing in the gentle wind, early in the morning. Kyrios Virgilio came, and some other fishermen, friends of Uncle Kristo. Not many could come, for the chapel was very tiny.

Kali and Aunt Maria had hurried to get there first in Uncle Kristo's boat. They wanted to sweep and clean, and put flowers on the altar. They had also brought the cakes that went with the celebration.

Oh, what a morning! The sky was blue. The sea was blue.

The sails of the fishing boats were blue. And everywhere there was translucent brightness, and into this light Maria and Kristo said their grateful prayer. "Thank you God, for our past happy ten years. Please be with us again, each day, until the end of our lives, and after."

Then they all sailed home.

Aunt Maria gave Kali a hug and said, "Never mind about yesterday. I'm sure you didn't mean to be bad."

They turned the lighthouse point, the blue sails filling with the wind, the long white beard of the priest flying out behind him, and the silvery-white beach of their home stretching all the way to their small white house in the dunes.

"O, do look!" Aunt Maria cried. "We have guests! There are people all around our house! I do hope we have enough cakes to go around."

"We have enough!" Uncle Kristo laughed aloud, he was so happy. "Kali and I went shopping all the way to Kymi yesterday. I have got you a real anniversary cake, my Maria!"

He steered his little boat, like a gay flying bird, right into the sands. Kyrios Malcolm and Kyria Bunty, and their visitors, and a lot of friends and relatives from the village and from the port on the other side of the island (that's why Uncle Kyrios had wanted to go there, to Linaria, the day before, to invite them,) were there. They waved, and then some of them waded into the sea to help Kali and Aunt Maria out of the boat.

They all cried, "MANY YEARS!" and they shouted, "May you live in happiness!" and a lot of other friendly greetings.

But Kali kept tugging at Aunt Maria. "Please, please," she said, "Come to the bedroom."

Aunt Maria was busy greeting people, but all the same she said, "I'll come right now, Kali, child."

There, above the chest, was the golden mirror, reflecting the light and the sea. It was big and clear and bright, and it had an immense carved golden frame.

Kyria Bunty had hung it up while they were at the chapel on the rock. (Uncle Kristo had secretly put the nail into the wall while Aunt Maria had been making the cakes.)

Aunt Maria burst into tears again. But these were happy tears. Then she made all the guests come into the room to see what her Kali had given her.

In the crowd, someone slipped a big parcel into Kali's hand. She looked up; it was Kyrios Malcolm. "If you had been a boy, you might have chosen this," he grinned. "You had some wages left over, you know."

Kali opened the parcel. It was the marvelous battery light Uncle Kristo needed for his boat.

She had never been so happy before.

It was a marvelous anniversary. There were so many good things to eat that everyone had to sleep after lunch. Later, those who wanted to went for a swim. The moon was rising before the last of the guests went home.

That night, under her pillow, Kali found a scarf. It was in all the colors of the sea and the sky and of a bright day. She kept it always.

And she never forgot what Achilles had told her.

64